W9-ATF-354

Easter Bunny Blues

by Carol Wallace

illustrated by

Steve Björkman

Holiday House / New York

To my grandnephew, Aden Kale Allen
C. W.

For Mia and Marley
S. B.

Reading level: 2.6

Text copyright © 2009 by Carol Wallace
Illustrations copyright © 2009 by Steve Björkman
All Rights Reserved
Printed and Bound in Malaysia
www.holidayhouse.com
First Edition
1 3 5 7 9 10 8 6 4 2

Library of Congress Cataloging-in-Publication Data
Wallace, Carol, 1948–
Easter Bunny blues / by Carol Wallace ; illustrated by
Steve Björkman. — 1st ed.
p. cm.
Summary: Although they do not have super powers like
the Easter Bunny, dogs Petey and Old Jack enlist the help
of their animal friends to decorate and deliver colorful
eggs to expectant children when the famed rabbit falls ill.
ISBN-13: 978-0-8234-2162-6 (hardcover)
1. Easter Bunny—Juvenile fiction. [1. Easter Bunny—Fiction.
2. Dogs—Fiction. 3. Animals—Fiction.] I. Björkman, Steve, ill.
II. Title.
PZ7.W15473Eas 2009
[Fic]—dc22
2007043621

Contents

Chapter 1
Clucking and Quacking

A commotion woke Petey
from his sleep.

"Quack, quack."

"Cluck, cluck."

Ears perked, the little dog ran
to the fence.

Old Jack was standing guard.

"What can you see?" Petey asked.
"The ducks and chickens must be
having a wild party," Old Jack said.
"The old hens are flapping their wings
and clucking at the ducks."

Six ducks waddled toward the dogs.

"What's going on?" Old Jack called.

"It's bad, really bad news,"
  said Yellow Duck.

"The Easter Bunny's got the flu,"
  Brown Duck said.

"Easter's a week away.

  What are we going to do?"
  asked Speckled Duck.

"What's the Easter Bunny?"
Petey asked Old Jack.
"The Easter Bunny is just
   a plain old rabbit most of the year,"
Old Jack said. "Right before Easter
he gets his superpowers
and creates spring magic."

"What's spring magic?" Petey asked.

"You were little last year.

But our girl Belle had so much fun.

The Easter Bunny left her

a lot of colorful Easter eggs.

She even found some candy ones,"

Old Jack explained.

Petey plopped down in his doghouse.

His ears drooped.

He thought about Belle.

"We've got to do something, Old Jack,"
  Petey said.

"I want Belle to be happy too."

"It's not just for her.

  Almost all children love

  the Easter Bunny," Old Jack said.

Chapter 2
A Plan

"What does the Easter Bunny do?"
Petey asked.

"The week before Easter,
Bunny gets his magic," Old Jack said.

"He collects eggs.
He decorates them in beautiful colors.
He delivers them in special baskets
to children everywhere."

"His powers must be really super to do that!" said Petey.

"The Easter Bunny is very special," Old Jack said. "He must really be sick or he would have gathered the eggs from the chickens and ducks."

"How can we help?" Petey asked.

"I don't know, Petey.
We don't have superpowers
like the Easter Bunny."
The commotion from the barn
started again.
The old hens were clucking about
the Easter Bunny.

"If we work together,
maybe *we* can get Easter
for Belle," said Petey.
Old Jack perked his ears. "How?"
"We can ask the ducks and
chickens for eggs.
The rabbits can bring them to us."
"We have lots of squirrels around here,"
Old Jack said. "They are messy,
but they can be very creative.
They have paintbrushes for tails."

"Paint! Where can we get paint?"
Petey squeaked.

"The birds can help," Old Jack answered.

"They can find berries
and fruits to mix together."

"What about the other dogs?
Can't they help?" asked Petey.

"Dogs are strong and very helpful,
but the people will notice
if they are missing,"
warned Old Jack.

"Oh dear!

I thought we had it all figured out."

"That's it! The deer," said Old Jack.

"They are fast.

They can take the eggs

to the rabbits around the world.

If we work at night,

no one will know the dogs

are missing from their homes."

"It's only a week until Easter,"

Petey said.

"We have to begin soon."

"But there is still a problem,"
said Old Jack. "Easter baskets.
We have to put the eggs in something.
The Easter Bunny is the only one
who knows where the baskets are!"
"Are you afraid of the flu?"
Petey asked.
"Of course not."
"Do you know where
the Easter Bunny lives?"
Old Jack perked his ears. "I think so."
"Let's go talk to him,"
Petey said.

Chapter 3
Easter Baskets

Old Jack started digging.
"I can scoot between the gate
and the fence.
I'll dig from the other side,"
said Petey.
"Go, Petey.
Get us out of here."

Dirt flying, the two dogs dug and dug.

Finally Old Jack squeezed his way free.

"Let's go find the Easter Bunny."

Old Jack shook the dirt from his coat.

The two friends trotted to the woods.

Old Jack's ears perked as he sniffed.

"Morning, Mrs. Bunny!"

Old Jack greeted her.

"Good morning to you, dogs.

What brings you to

this part of the woods?"

she asked.

"We heard that

the Easter Bunny

has the flu,"

Petey said.

"He's been pretty sick.

He's got the blues too."

Mrs. Bunny wiped her paws

on her apron.

"We're here to help.
We have an idea
to get the eggs decorated
and sent to kids all over the world.
But we don't know
where the baskets are,"
Old Jack explained.

"I'll talk to Clarence
    and see what he can do.
    He will be thankful for your help,"
    Mrs. Bunny said.
"Work starts in the meadow
    tomorrow night,"
    said Old Jack.

The next day Petey and Old Jack
went to the meadow.

Baskets were stacked all around.

Piles of eggs filled the hay field.

Chickens and ducks carried
dozens more.

Tails flicked as the squirrels
scurried around.

"Squawk!" Jay Bird called.

Petey jumped.

"Who's in charge here?"

Jay Bird stared at Petey.

"We've worked hard
to get these colors right."

The evening sky was filled
with birds carrying
berries in their beaks.

"Jay Bird!
   Can you talk to the crows
   about relaying the baskets
   to the next meadow?"
   Old Jack called.
   "I'll tell them," Jay Bird said.

Chapter 4
Spring Magic

For five nights the animals
worked hard.
The early birds rolled
the eggs to the geese.
The geese lined up
the eggs.

Tails swishing, the squirrels
splattered paint.
Fluffing their feathers,
the chickens dried them.
The ducks rolled the eggs
to waiting baskets.

The field rabbits lined up to give
the eggs to the deer and dogs.
The deer delivered them
to the rabbits in far-off meadows.
Jay Bird swooped in. "Work faster."
"We've been working as fast as we can,"
Petey said.
"There's just one night to finish,"
Jay Bird said.

Suddenly, everything got quiet
in the meadow.
A shadow covered the ground
as a huge bunny walked into the field.

The chickens and ducks were silent.

The rabbits hid in the grass.

The deer and dogs dropped

their baskets.

Except for their tails,

the squirrels were perfectly still.

Petey and Old Jack stared.

"Easter Bunny! Do you still have the flu?"

"Look at me!
I beat the blues.
My magical powers are back!"
the Easter Bunny said.
Cheers shot out from the meadow.
"We've been working hard,
but we are still a little bit short,"
Old Jack said.
"You've done a wonderful job.
Now that I'm here
we can get this done in a flash,"
the Easter Bunny said.

The Easter Bunny raised his arms
and the meadow filled
with bright lights
and beautiful colors.
Instantly, baskets loaded
with Easter surprises
appeared in the field.

"Hooray!" everyone cheered.

"Wow! You didn't need us after all,"
Petey said.

"Oh yes, I did," the Easter Bunny said.
"There is no way that I could have
completed all this.
While I finish these last deliveries,
I have a treat for you
and all your friends."
The Easter Bunny threw his paws
in the air.
The meadow filled
with Easter surprises
for everyone.

The workers all shouted.

"Three cheers for the Easter Bunny!"

The Easter Bunny answered,

"You helped make Easter this year.

We did it together!"